D1177431

A Note to Parents and Caregivers:

Read-it! Readers are for children who are just starting on the amazing road to reading. These beautiful books support both the acquisition of reading skills and the love of books.

 The PURPLE LEVEL presents basic topics and objects using high frequency words and simple language patterns.

 The RED LEVEL presents familiar topics using common words and repeating sentence patterns.

 The BLUE LEVEL presents new ideas using a larger vocabulary and varied sentence structure.

 The YELLOW LEVEL presents more challenging ideas, a broad vocabulary, and wide variety in sentence structure.

 The GREEN LEVEL presents more complex ideas, an extended vocabulary range, and expanded language structures.

 The ORANGE LEVEL presents a wide range of ideas and concepts using challenging vocabulary and complex language structures.

When sharing a book with your child, read in short stretches, pausing often to talk about the pictures. Have your child turn the pages and point to the pictures and familiar words. And be sure to reread favorite stories or parts of stories.

There is no right or wrong way to share books with children. Find time to read with your child, and pass on the legacy of literacy.

Adria F. Klein, Ph.D.
Professor Emeritus
California State University
San Bernardino, California

Editor: Nick Healy
Designer: Nathan Gassman
Page Production: Lori Bye
Creative Director: Keith Griffin
Editorial Director: Carol Jones
The illustrations in this book were created digitally.

Picture Window Books
5115 Excelsior Boulevard
Suite 232
Minneapolis, MN 55416
877-845-8392
www.picturewindowbooks.com

Printed in the United States of America.

Library of Congress Cataloging-in-Publication Data
Dougherty, Terri.
The camping scare / by Terri Dougherty ; illustrated by Jeffrey Thompson.
p. cm. — (Read-it! readers)
Summary: When Beth and Ben go camping in their backyard, a strange thumping
noise keeps them awake.
ISBN-13: 978-1-4048-2405-8 (hardcover)
ISBN-10: 1-4048-2405-7 (hardcover)
[1. Camping—Fiction. 2. Noise—Fiction. 3. Hispanic Americans—Fiction.]
I. Thompson, Jeffrey (Jeffrey Allen), 1970- , ill. II. Title. III. Series.
PZ7.D74436Cam 2006
[E]—dc22   2006003441

The Camping Scare

by Terri Dougherty

illustrated by Jeffrey Thompson

Special thanks to our advisers for their expertise:

Adria F. Klein, Ph.D.
Professor Emeritus, California State University
San Bernardino, California

Susan Kesselring, M.A.
Literacy Educator
Rosemount–Apple Valley–Eagan (Minnesota) School District

PiCTURE WiNDOW BOOKS
Minneapolis, Minnesota

Ben and Ben went camping in their backyard.

...rk summer night.

They set up an old brown te

They ate fluffy marshmallows

6

They told scary stories.

Finally, they crawled into their sleeping bags. But they could not get to sleep.

Ben and Beth heard a sound.

THUMP
THUD THUD

9

Ben's heart pounded. Beth's heart raced.

Ben and Beth plugged their ears.
They hummed a song. But they
could still hear the sound.

"I don't know," Ben said.

The thumping got faster and faster.

Then, the noise stopped. Ben's heart still pounded. Beth's heart still raced.

Beth and Ben peeked out of the tent. A light went on in the house.

18

The back door slid open. Mom set
two orange shoes onto the step.

"My shoes!" said Beth. "I asked Mom to wash them."

20

"Then she must have dried them," said Ben. "The shoes in the dryer made all that noise."

"Mystery solved," said Beth.

"Now it's time for bed," said Ben.
"But let's keep the light on."

More *Read-it!* Readers

Bright pictures and fun stories help you practice your
reading skills. Look for more books at your level.

At the Beach 1-4048-0651-2
Bears on Ice 1-4048-1577-5
The Bossy Rooster 1-4048-0051-4
Dust Bunnies 1-4048-1168-0
Emily's Pictures 1-4048-2409-X
Flying with Oliver 1-4048-1583-X
Frog Pajama Party 1-4048-1170-2
Galen's Camera 1-4048-1610-0
Jack's Party 1-4048-0060-3
Last in Line 1-4048-2415-4
The Lifeguard 1-4048-1584-8
Mike's Night-light 1-4048-1726-3
Nate the Dinosaur 1-4048-1728-X
The Playground Snake 1-4048-0556-7
Recycled! 1-4048-0068-9
Robin's New Glasses 1-4048-1587-2
The Sassy Monkey 1-4048-0058-1
Tuckerbean 1-4048-1591-0
What's Bugging Pamela? 1-4048-1189-3

Looking for a specific title or level? A complete list
of *Read-it!* Readers is available on our Web site:
www.picturewindowbooks.com